Let's Keep Our Oceans, Rivers, and Lakes Clean

by
Richard D. Covey
& Diane H. Pappas

Illustrated by
The Pixel Factory

SCHOLASTIC INC.
New York Toronto London Auckland Sydney
Mexico City New Delhi Hong Kong Buenos Aires

To John, Casey, and Nikos — may you always enjoy clear oceans.
Love, R.D.C. & D.H.P.

Special thanks to the talented artists of The Pixel Factory,
Willie Castro, Desma Thompson, & Bob Duane

———————————————————

ISBN-13: 978-0-545-06105-6
ISBN-10: 0-545-06105-9

12 11 10 9 8 7 6 5 4 3 2 1   9 10 11 12 13 14/0

Printed in the U.S.A.
First printing, March 2009

MEET THE KID GUARDIANS

From their home base in the mystical Himalayan mountain kingdom of Shambala, Zak the Yak and the Kid Guardians are always on alert, ready to protect the children of the world from danger.

 ZAK THE YAK is a gentle giant with a heart of gold. He's the leader of the Kid Guardians.

 Loyal and lovable, **SCRUBBER** is Zak's best friend and sidekick.

 BUZZER is both street-smart and book-smart, with a real soft spot for kids.

 Always curious about the world, **SMOOCH** loves to meet new people and see new places.

 CARROT, with her wild red hair, is funny, lovable, and the first to jump in when help is needed.

 Whenever a child is in danger, the **TROUBLE BUBBLE**™ sounds an alarm and then instantly transports the Kid Guardians to that location.

"Welcome back, Stan. So glad you're better," Ms. Bronstein said. "Tell us what happened to you at Benson Beach."

Stan replied, "After boogie-boarding all morning, the water upset my stomach, and made my eyes and throat sting."

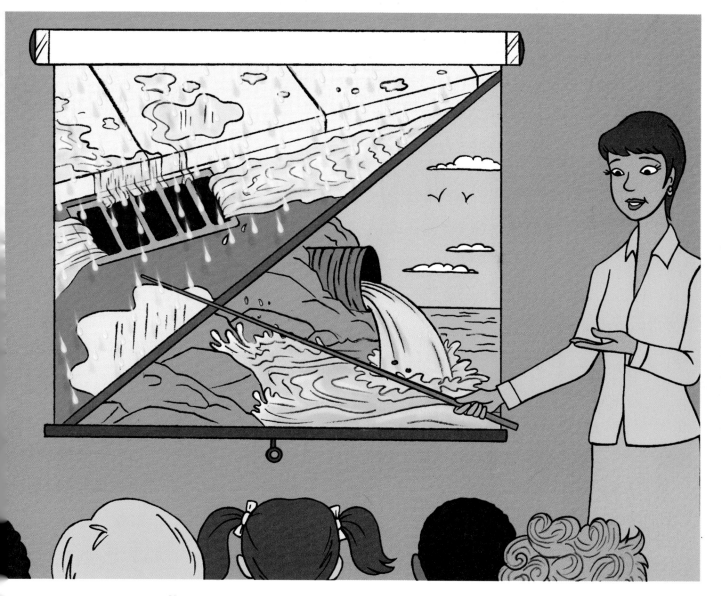

"Most water pollution is caused by things people do every day," explained Ms. Bronstein. "For example, cars leak oil onto streets, and people throw garbage in the gutter. Then rainwater washes everything through storm drains to the ocean or rivers."

"Carrot, we can help Ms. Bronstein. Come on, let's get going," said Zak.

"Hi, Zak," Ms. Bronstein said happily. "Kids, say hello to Zak the Yak, leader of the Kid Guardians, and Carrot."

"Hi," said Zak. "Together, we can learn what causes water pollution. Then you can teach others."

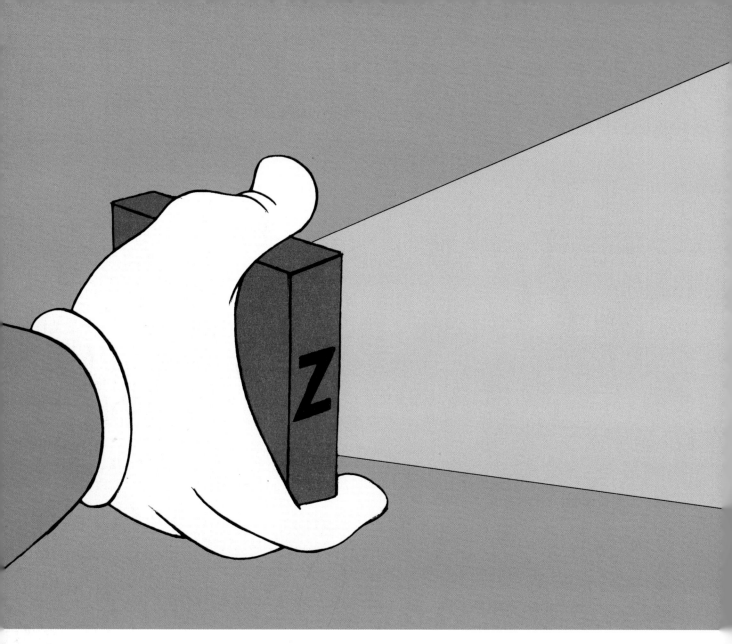

"Ships carrying oil across oceans can have accidents, and spill gallons and gallons of oil," Zak explained. "The oil kills thousands of birds and sea life. Look how Carrot saved some penguins."

"I saved this baby penguin just in time," said Carrot. "Her feathers were full of oil and she couldn't stay warm. When she tried to lick off the oil she became very sick."

"More than 70% of the earth is covered by oceans," explained Zak. "Most of the pollution caused by people ends up on the beaches near cities."

"Polluted water makes fish and other water animals sick," Carrot explained. "Sometimes creatures leave the area, and sometimes they die."

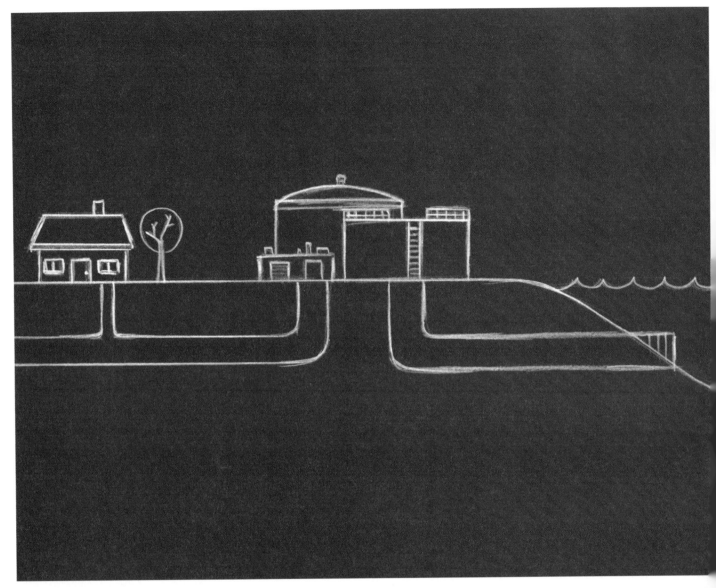

"Sewer pipes bring dirty water from toilets, washing machines, and garbage disposals to a treatment plant. After the water is cleaned, it goes into the ocean or river," said Zak.

"But some businesses are careless," said Zak. "They use fresh lake water to make their products. Then they dump chemicals and dirty wastewater back into the lakes. This makes fish sick, and we can't eat them because they'll make *us* sick."

Keeping Our Oceans, Rivers, and Lakes Clean

1. Check the car for oil leaks.

2. Always pick up after your dog.

3. Always throw trash in trash cans.

4. Never pour anything into the street. Eventually, it will wind up in the oceans, rivers, or lakes.

"Here are important ways you can all help reduce the pollution to our oceans, rivers, and, lakes," said Zak.

Project Ideas

Form a clean-up contest for Benson Beach—the team picking up the most trash wins.

Write a classroom letter to a local newspaper explaining ocean pollution and how to help clean up our oceans.

Design a class project to paint a mural of underwater ocean or lake floor showing pollution.

"Before Zak and Carrot leave, let's decide which of these projects our class should choose," announced Ms. Bronstein.

"These are all excellent ideas," said Carrot. "Whatever you choose will be a great decision."

"Remember, kids," Zak said, "you are all truly important in keeping our oceans, lakes, and rivers clean for the future. Please remember what you learned today. You will make a big difference to our world by reducing pollution."